I0570555

James Howard Kunstler

Manhattan Gothic

A Ghoulish Tale of Friendship and Tribulation

————

ALSO BY JAMES HOWARD KUNSTLER

Fiction

A Safe and Happy Place

The World Made By Hand Series
The Harrows of Spring
A History of the Future
The Witch of Hebron
World Made By Hand

Maggie Darling, a Modern Romance
Thunder Island
The Halloween Ball
The Hunt
Blood Solstice
An Embarrassment of Riches
The Life of Byron Jaynes
A Clown in the Moonlight
The Wampanaki Tales.

Nonfiction

Too Much Magic
The Long Emergency
The City in Mind
Home From Nowhere
The Geography of Nowhere

James Howard Kunstler

Manhattan Gothic

A Ghoulish Tale of Friendship and Tribulation

A Novella

———————

The Greenaway Series
Book Four

Highbrow Press

Copyright © 2021 by James Howard Kunstler

All rights reserved. No part of this book may be produced in any form or by electronic or mechanical means, including information storage and retrieval systems, without permission in writing from the publisher, except by a reviewer who may quote brief passages in a review. Scanning, uploading, and electronic distribution of this book, or the facilitation of such without the permission of the publisher is prohibited. Please purchase only authorized electronic editions, and do not participate in or encourage electronic piracy of copyrighted materials. Your support of the author's rights is appreciated. Any member of educational institutions wishing to photocopy part or all of the work for classroom use, or anthology, should send inquiries to Highbrow Books, PO Box 193, Saratoga Springs, New York 12866.

Published in the United States of America

ISBN: 978-0-9846252-3-9

Highbrow Press
PO Box 193
Saratoga Springs
New York, 12866

Years ago in New York City, an eleven-year-old boy named Jeff Greenaway conceived an inordinate fascination with a local television personality who went by the name of Count Zackuloff. The Count was the host of a regular horror movie program broadcast on Friday nights. His job was to introduce the movies and lead into the numerous commercial advertisements. He appeared in make-up derived from Lon Chaney's classic *Phantom of the Opera* guise, his skin ghoulishly whitened, eye sockets and nostrils shaded black, and hair parted slickly down the middle. His costume was a moldy black frock coat with a boiled shirtfront and, in place of a necktie, a large bejeweled medal worn at the throat, which he called "the Royal Transylvanian Star of Skull-duggery — with three tana leaf clusters."

The Count had been on the air about a year when Jeff and his chums in Mrs. Snipes's class at Public School No. 6 started tuning into the show on a regular basis.

"Did you catch the Count last night?" Jeff rang up his best friend Bobby Schindler each Saturday during those first rapturous weeks of discovery.

"Yeah. What a nut. The movie stunk, though."

The film in question had been *White Zombie* with Bela Lugosi.

"Can't he at least get something scary?" Bobby added. *"The Crawling Eye. The Night of the Blood Beast?"*

"Who cares about the movie?" Jeff retorted. "The movie isn't the point!"

Jeff was quite correct, of course, because as far as the Count himself was concerned, the worse the movie, the more opportunity there was for him to perform his antics, which became steadily more elaborate and outlandish from one broadcast to the next. His duties, strictly defined, were to greet the viewing audience, tell them a little about the picture, and serve as a buffer between the many ads for nasal spray and scenes of mummies lurching across the misty moors. At first, he was little more than a talking head. After the first few weeks on the air, however, he began to get up from his medieval-looking chair and move around. Then, one Friday night, he suddenly occupied a theatrical set, a sort of pasteboard dungeon. In the weeks that followed, he acquired a collection of nifty props, some of which took on lives of their own as supporting players.

For instance, there was his "wife" Hortense, whom the audience never actually saw because she "lived" in a packing crate from which wafted great plumes of glycerin stage-smoke, accompanied by a lot of eerie gurgling sound effects. A portrait of their domestic life soon developed. Hortense, the audience learned, was one of the Count's many "experiments." He would make cheeky remarks into the packing crate and little blobs of gelatinous goop would fly angrily up in reply. Then there was their "son" Janos, a stuffed dummy draped in rags who would fly across the top of the set on a wire — "home for the weekend from Transylvania University" —never remaining on screen long enough for the audience to make out what he looked like, and who communicated only in shrieks, barks, sobs, grunts and maniacal giggles.

By the fall of the year that concerns us, *Count Zackuloff's Midnight Mystery Theater* had fully evolved and entered the classic phase of its brief broadcast life. Thus, as Halloween drew near, the Count's popularity among the "boys and ghouls" of Mrs. Snipes's class soared to new heights. But no one was quite as obsessed with the antic figure in black-and-white as Jeff Greenaway. He plastered photographs clipped from *Famous Monsters of Filmland Magazine* all over his room in the apartment on East 79th Street. He stuck a pillow inside his pajamas and reenacted the famous rescue-of-Esmeralda scene from *The Hunchback of Notre Dame*, hollering "sanctuary!" at his parents (who represented the Parisian rabble) from the top of the living room sofa. He published a two-page mimeographed newspaper called *The Transylvania Times* in which the gala doings of the celebrated undead were chronicled in minute detail. He spent his allowance on greasepaint, nose putty, rubber scars and plastic fangs, which he bought at a little specialty shop in Times Square. Nobody in class 6-B had more sheer, detailed knowledge on matters beyond the grave than Jeff Greenaway, to whom the werewolves, vampires, mummies, zombies, the accursed, the misbegotten and the shrunken or overgrown survivors of atom bomb blasts were all beloved members of an extended family.

Now, it happened one Friday in mid-October, that one of Jeff's father's law partners had to give up a pair of highly coveted tickets to the smash Broadway musical *How to Succeed in Business Without Really Trying*. And because the tickets were so hard to get, and the seats right in Orchestra Row G, and on the aisle, too, Jeff's father simply couldn't *not* accept them. And it also happened that the regular babysitter, a spinster named Alma Grosbeck, was not available on such short notice, nor were any of her sometime replacements. It was going on seven o'clock. The show had an eight o'clock curtain. And therefore, in desperation, Jeff's mother entered his room — his "tomb," as he called it — and extracted the following promise.

"If we trust you to stay at home without a babysitter tonight, like a grown-up, do you promise to be a good boy?"

Secretly the idea electrified him.

"Don't worry, Mom. I won't burn the building down."

She stooped down to where he was sitting at his desk, bracelets jangling and a nimbus of perfume enveloping her.

"What are you working on, Pussycat?" she inquired.

"Just a little experiment," Jeff replied. Actually, he was fashioning a miniature guillotine out of his Erector Set, using one of his father's Gillette Blue Blades for the business end, but at this stage it was just a hodgepodge of as-yet-unassembled parts on the desktop.

"There are cookies in the cabinet and ice cream in the fridge," she said, kissing him on the cheek and petting his head.

"There always is, Mom."

"We'll be home around midnight. Remember, be good."

His father appeared in the doorway, adjusting the black bowtie of his tuxedo.

"You heard your mother now," he said, smiling good-naturedly, then, stealing a glance at his wristwatch added, "Gosh, Hon, we'd better shake a leg."

Jeff escorted them to the door and double-locked it behind them as they requested. He waited for the sound of the elevator to bear them away and, when he was sure they were gone, he nearly bounded off the walls of the apartment he was so delirious with glee. For an idea in the form of a wish had been taking shape in his mind over many weeks, and here, all of a sudden, was the opportunity to act on it. That idea was to go down to the television studio from which *Count Zacku-loff's Midnight Mystery Theater* was broadcast and to personally meet the Great Ghoul himself. The reason he had not attempted it until now was simply that he hadn't been able to think up a plausible excuse to stay out on a Friday night after eight-o'clock, which was as late as he was allowed to visit at his friends' apartments. He happened to know exactly where the Channel Five studio was (67th Street off Third Avenue). As editor-in-chief of *The Transylvania Times*, he had even appeared there once after school, to inquire as to when the Count arrived ("around ten" the receptionist told him, snapping her chewing gum, "when he's sober").

The opportunity presented by his parents' night at the theater left only two logistical matters unsettled: what to wear? And how to get out of the building without being noticed by the doorman?

He had a couple of hours to agonize over it before setting off for the studio. At first, he considered donning one of the scary monster disguises he had lately created, in hope of impressing his hero. He even began gluing on a few scars and a fake eye in the middle of his forehead. But this, he suspected, might draw unwanted attention to himself en route, and it occurred to him that a "normal" appearance might get him past the receptionist more easily.

Leaving his building unnoticed, on the other hand, proved to be a cinch. There was the delivery entrance off the basement. The freight elevator was shut down at night, but the basement was accessible via the fire stairs. It was simply a matter of putting some electrical tape — from his dad's toolbox — over the delivery door's lock to get back in. And so, at a quarter to ten, dressed neatly in a blue blazer and stripped tie, so as to appear professional, Jeff left the phone off the hook in the apartment and slipped out into the spooky metropolitan night.

"You're who?" the receptionist asked testily, still snapping her gum. Jeff had told her that he was Count Zackuloff's nephew, Renfield, from England.

"You don't sound like you're from England," she observed. "Is that your first name or last?"

He wasn't sure, but he ventured that it was his first. Eyeing him suspiciously, she flipped a lever on her switchboard and muttered into her headset.

"He'll be down in a minute," she reported.

The thrill that coursed through Jeff was at once eclipsed by panic. The Count was coming down? To see him? What would he say? Why hadn't he thought about what to say beforehand? Now it was too late. He couldn't think. Maybe he should just apologize for bothering him—

Just then, an elevator door opened, and there stood the exalted figure himself, his glowering powdery visage so pale compared to the cocoa-brown face of the elevator man. He was not yet in costume, but rather wore a somewhat tattered old black and red satin smoking jacket over a pair of khaki trousers and oxblood loafers without socks. A triangle of white undershirt could be seen where he usually wore the Royal Transylvanian Star of Skullduggery.

He strode forward across the lobby, arms crossed imperiously, and glared down at Jeff. To Jeff, the Count appeared almost as tall as King Kong. In fact, he was six-foot-four.

"Renfield, my boy!" he suddenly cried, throwing open his spidery arms and sweeping Jeff into an embrace. "What a treat to see you after all these centuries!" He stepped back from the stupefied Jeff and pinched one of his cheeks. "Looks like they haven't been feeding you enough flies and spiders at the asylum. Come up to the dungeon with me and I'll rustle you up a few, ha ha!" he said, adding his ghoulish trademark laugh.

After a brief elevator ride, there Jeff was, standing right in the middle of the Count's set. The fact that its stone walls were flimsy painted flats made it no less impressive. With more than an hour remaining until airtime, the studio was half-darkened and the huge TV cameras and microphone booms sat idle.

"Well, what do you think?" the Count asked.

"It's . . . incredible."

"Want to sit on my throne for a while?"

"C-c-could I?"

Jeff ran over to the big wooden chair with its gargoyle armrests. Meanwhile, the Count threw a switch and a whole bank of lights came on blindingly overhead. Jeff could feel the heat radiate off them.

"That's what it's like to be me," the Count said.

"Can I peek inside Hortense's box?" Jeff asked, shielding his eyes.

"Sure, go ahead."

He warily approached the packing crate and threw open the hinged lid. To his distress, it was absolutely empty.

"Where is she?"

"On sab-bat-ical," the Count said with a snort, but Jeff didn't get the gag.

He did, however, succeed in getting a close look at Janos, who turned out, a little disappointingly, to be a dressmaker's dummy under a torn, paint-smeared flannel nightshirt, with a rubber "caveman" mask pinned to the head. Altogether, Jeff spent about fifteen minutes browsing around the props before the Count glanced at his watch and said, "Isn't it kind of late for a little insectivore like yourself to be prowling the dark underside of Gotham?"

"Pardon me?"

"Your mummy's probably worried to death about you, ha ha!"

"She doesn't know I'm here."

"What!"

"I snuck out of the apartment to come down here."

"Quick, come with me."

Rather like Mr. Kreevich, the assistant principal and chief disciplinarian at P.S. Six, the Count stiffly marched Jeff back down to the lobby.

"Get this little monster a cab," he said to the security guard. "Have you got any money, kid?"

Jeff felt in his pocket and drew out eighty-seven cents.

"Christ, that's not enough."

"It's okay, I'll take the bus."

"Here." The Count pulled a crumpled bill out of his trouser pocket and handed it to Jeff. "You take a cab straight home," he said sternly. Jeff was about to apologize for coming down without permission when the Count added, "And meet me here next Friday after school. We'll have some fun together, okay?"

"Okay," Jeff nodded, though bewildered.

"Next Friday."

"Taxi's here," the security guard said.

"Bon voyage for now, then, Renfield," the Count said, with a maniacal laugh as the security guard escorted Jeff out the door.

He got back to the apartment via the delivery entrance well before his parents returned from the theater and a late supper at Sardi's, and in plenty of time to catch the beginning of *Count Zackuloff's Midnight Mystery Theater*.

"You must have been on the phone for two hours straight," his mother complained, finding him awake at half past midnight watching the thrilling climax of *Mr. Wang, Detective* starring Boris Karloff. "Every time I called there was a busy signal!"

"Hey, at least you knew I was here," Jeff said without taking his gaze off the screen.

"That's true."

"And I didn't burn the building down."

"Well, don't stay up too late, Pussycat."

"No school tomorrow, Mom," he reminded her.

The only disappointing thing was that he couldn't tell her about the incredibly wondrous meeting with his idol. Of course, he told Bobby Schindler the next day when the two of them went out to ride their bikes around Central Park, but Bobby reacted with an air of strange detachment as though he not only disbelieved Jeff, but also worried a little about his sanity. Jeff sensed Bobby's incredulity and decided not to mention that their idol had actually invited him back to the TV studio next Friday.

"That movie sure stunk, though," Bobby said as they wheeled past the Egyptian obelisk behind the Metropolitan Museum of Art. "Hey, if you happen to see the Count again, ask him to put something decent on for a change. Something with real monsters in it, like *The Lost Continent*."

"Okay, I'll ask him."

Jeff didn't breathe another word about the amazing encounter all week long, nor brag about it to anyone else at P.S. Six because, amongst their own kind, children are the world's most thoroughgoing skeptics. Instead, he quietly endured six days of the most piquant anticipation, worrying more and more whether, perhaps, the

Count told him to come back on Friday just as a ruse to get rid of him — only somehow that didn't make sense, not even to Jeff, who knew a thing or two about how grown-ups' minds worked.

Finally, the great day arrived. Time crept by so slowly that he felt as though he were serving a life sentence in the sixth grade. At three o'clock, when the bell rang and the liberated children roistered under the sycamore trees along Madison Avenue, there was some talk among Jeff's circle of friends about going over to Bobby Schindler's penthouse on 73rd Street to lob water balloons off the terrace. But Jeff pretended he had a dental appointment and caught a bus downtown.

All the way down Madison, past the art galleries and the expensive little shops, Jeff worried about what lay in store for him. By the time he got to the TV studio he had convinced himself that he was in for a scene of humiliation, that the gum-chewing receptionist would laugh in his face and say, *The Count? He doesn't even come down here 'til ten o'clock, you little boob.* But she wasn't on duty. A redhead of apparently better breeding sat in her place, and when Jeff mumbled his reason for being there, she smiled and said brightly, "Oh yes. Go right up to his office on the fifth floor. He's waiting for you."

"Ah, Renfield, my little bug-eyed friend," the Count greeted him warmly from the office doorway. Jeff was startled to hear the familiar voice coming from a face without makeup that looked so utterly unrecognizable. It was the face of, say, a graduate student of a literary bent, thin, but with good bones, an intelligent mouth, and sad, slightly rheumy eyes behind a pair of horn-rimmed spectacles. The longish dark brown hair could have benefitted from having a comb run through it, and the natural part was on the left, not down the center.

"God, you're so young," Jeff helplessly blurted out.

The Count himself seemed momentarily dismayed, but quickly recollected himself. "I guess three hundred and ninety-four *is* a bit young — for a vampire! Ha ha! Won't you come into my mausoleum."

Jeff entered the windowless cubicle, perhaps

ten feet square, a room hardly bigger than his mother's walk-in closet. The walls were strangely bare, except for a nude magazine centerfold over the face of which the Count had pasted a newspaper photo of Jackie Kennedy. The only furniture in the room was a dressing table littered with tubes of greasepaint and a coat tree from which hung Zack's familiar costume as well as the tattered satin smoking jacket. Just now, the Count was attired in khaki pants, loafers, and a plain white T-shirt. This, too, unnerved Jeff because it was exactly the way his counselor at Camp Timahoe, Bob Waring, used to dress on Parents' Day.

"Look what I've got for you, my little homunculus," the Count said as he reached into a cardboard carton and pulled out a record album. On the cover was the Count in full regalia, his visage tinged greenish as he leaned smilingly over a chemical laboratory table arrayed with simmering retorts of colored liquids. The album was titled *Spook Along With Zack*. It contained twelve songs, all on Transylvanian themes — "The Mummy's Love Cry," "Rock Around the Crypt," "Waltz of the Werewolves," et cetera.

"Wow!" Jeff gasped. "Can we listen to it?"

"All in good time. First, let's get you into make-up."

Why it was necessary to put on make-up, the Count didn't say, but Jeff could only imagine that, somehow, he had won the job of playing Janos on the show, replacing the flying dummy. And the prospect of becoming an actual TV star overnight was so amazing that he didn't want to even ask and risk being disappointed. He could just picture all the other kids at P.S. Six swarming around him as he arrived for school on Monday. Would they ask for his autograph? The idea gave him the shivers.

It took the Count ten minutes to make up Jeff's face as a junior version of his. Then he put his own make-up on and changed into the moldy black suit. As the finishing touch, they both combed their hair parted down the middle with a kind of hair tonic that turned stiff when it dried. Jeff was reassured to see the Count looking normal again.

"I have all these neat scars and this eye that I can glue onto the middle of my forehead," Jeff told him excitedly.

"You look perfect just the way you are," the Count said. "Perfectly dreadful. Now, what do you say we go have some fun?"

"Gee. Sure."

But instead of heading into the studio — for some sort of rehearsal, Jeff assumed — they took the elevator down to the lobby and all of a sudden Jeff found himself walking up 67th Street, practically jogging to keep up with his idol's long-legged stride.

"Hey, where are we going?"

"You'll see," the Count said.

They took a left on Third Avenue and marched downtown past the boutiques and many antique stores full of brass beds and crystal chandeliers. People stared at the strange duo, naturally, but no more so than they might at a pair of U.N. diplomats dressed in the odd raiment of their native land. A few cars honked at them. As they approached Bloomingdale's department store, the crowds on the sidewalk grew thicker and Jeff struggled to keep up as the Count strode confidently forward, humming a tune off his record. Finally, they reached 57th Street. The Count turned right at the corner. Halfway up the block to Lexington Avenue, he stopped in front of the Horn and Hardart Automat.

"Here we are!" he announced and ushered the breathless Jeff into a revolving door.

They took trays, got change from the central cashier in her ornate kiosk, and went browsing among the little display windows of casseroles, sandwiches, pies and other goodies that made dining at the Automat such a scintillating adventure. The Count dropped 15 nickels into a slot for his ramekin of Hungarian goulash. Jeff selected a cheese Danish (five nickels), for which his mentor insisted on paying. They repaired to the hot beverage counter for coffee and hot cocoa. Finally, the Count selected a table for them at the absolute center of the enormous cafeteria.

"Mmmmm," the Count said, smacking his thin lips and bellowing theatrically, "looks almost as good as Mom's blood pudding."

Though it was four o'clock in the afternoon, the Automat was quite busy, and its many patrons regarded the Count and his little protűgű as a sort of teatime entertainment, tittering, gaping or shaking their heads at the goofiness of metropolitan life. Jeff was not sure he enjoyed so much attention.

"Where do you go to school, Renfield?" the Count said, loudly, as though playing to the whole room.

"P.S. 6 on 82nd and Madison—" Jeff said as an elderly woman in a dusty blue overcoat approached their table. She wore a kerchief over her head in the old-world style, had eyeglasses in cat's eye frames with lenses so thick they made her eyeballs look twice life-size, and was afflicted with a large hairy mole on her chin. She advanced on them warily, with a bashful smile, clutching a worn brown purse to her shapeless bosom.

"I haff seen you," she declared to the Count, wagging a blunt finger at him playfully. "You are on the telefision, yes?"

"Auntie Zebna!" the Count exclaimed. He fairly sprang from his seat and embraced the crone, who stood nearly two feet shorter than him. A hush fell over the automat. Forks were put down. "Yes, ladies and gentlemen" — the Count now addressed the room at large — "here she is, my dear old Auntie Zebna from Bucharest! Why, it's been over three hundred years."

The old woman, who could not escape the Count's clutches, blushed and made *aw, go on* gestures with her right hand while trying to push him away with her left.

"Yes, it was she who raised me from a little baby bat, who rocked me in my casket as the werewolves howled on our dreary old Carpathian mountainside!"

He planted a big slushy kiss on her cheek, right above the fearsome mole. She uttered a cry in some incomprehensible Slavic tongue and, as the Count finally let her go, waddled away beaming and shaking her head.

Jeff could barely reflect on his own gathering mortification when the Count stood up, broke into song, and performed a little soft shoe dance — another number off his album, "The Zombie Shuffle." A brisk round of applause from the crowd rather surprised Jeff. In his experience, grownups were more apt to remain stonily silent in the face of such a public disturbance (while presumably waiting for the police to arrive). The Automat had taken on the festive air of a nightclub.

When the Count returned to his seat, a few patrons came over to ask for his autograph, and then several more, and soon a dozen others formed a line behind them. The Count happily scrawled his flamboyant signature across scraps of paper and copies of the Daily Mirror, informing each fan about his new album and asking them to tune into his TV show. He introduced Jeff as his nephew Renfield, from Transylvania, and Jeff too signed autographs. As he got caught up in the excitement, his embarrassment ebbed and he came to realize that the Count's zany capers were not those of a common lunatic, but rather of a shrewd self-promoter. He felt a little ashamed of himself for doubting his hero and threw himself into what remained of the publicity stunt with his whole heart and soul, putting on an accent like Bela Lugosi's and chatting with the autograph hounds — all adults, by the way — about various doings back in Transylvania (the mummy's strike, the new blood bank, the peasants' garlic festival).

By five o'clock, with the dinner crowd swarming in the Automat, and the line of autograph seekers more than replenishing itself, the Count called it quits. ("Always leave 'em wanting more," he whispered to Jeff.) In a little while, they were back uptown in the studio.

"God, that was great, Zack," Jeff said as he and the Count removed their make-up with cold cream. Suddenly, a man about Jeff's father's age appeared in the doorway. His nervous, gloomy demeanor was evident in the way he dragged fiercely on a cigarette.

"What's this I hear about you in the Automat?" he asked tersely.

"Oh, hi, Phil," the Count said.

"I want to see you in my office in five minutes," Phil said. The cigarette plugged into his reddened face looked like a fuse, Jeff thought, and he half expected Phil's head to blow up. Then the man vanished.

"Who was that?" Jeff whispered.

"Phil Torgesen, the program director."

"He seemed kind of ticked off."

"He's always ticked off," the Count said, wiping the cold cream off with a wad of tissues.

"I think he was born ticked off."

"You're not gonna get fired, are you?"

"Fired?" the Count cackled at the idea. "Well, I guess you'd better run along now, Renfield. Don't forget your record album."

"Hey, Zack, can you do me a favor?"

"I don't know. What?"

"Can you play that movie *The Lost Continent* tonight?"

"Hmmm. Caesar Romero and the dinosaurs?"

"Yeah, that's the one."

"I'll see what I can do."

"God, that would be great. Well, maybe I'll see you again some time, huh?"

"You bet," the Count said, giving him a playful tap on the shoulder. "By the way, what's your real name, Renfield?"

Jeff told him, then asked, "What's yours?"

"Zack."

"No, really?"

"Well, Zachary. Zachary Orloff. Get it: Count Zackuloff?"

"Jeez. . ."

"Say, write down your phone number, kid. Maybe there's some way we can fit you in around here."

"God, you mean it?"

"Sure."

Jeff scrawled his number on a proffered memo pad, then made to leave. "Hey, good luck with Mr. Torgesen," he said.

"Don't worry about him. If all else fails, I'll drive a wooden stake through his heart — that is, if he's got one." The Count guffawed at his own joke and Jeff could hear his hero's demented laughter all the way down the hall to the elevator.

That evening, Jeff called Bobby Schindler to tell him about his amazing excursion to the Automat — which was greeted with the utmost skepticism — and also the fabulous news that the Count had a record album coming out.

"I know," Bobby said. "I bought one on the way home."

"Where'd you get a hold of it?"

"At the record store, where else?"

"He didn't say it was out already."

"It's out. Anybody can buy one."

"He gave me a free copy."

"Sure."

"It's autographed."

"By you, I bet."

"Okay. You don't believe me? Just wait until tonight. I made a special request to show *The Lost Continent* tonight and he said he would."

"The TV guide says he's showing *The Devil Bat*."

"You just wait and see."

"*TV Guide* never lies," Bobby said snootily.

As things turned out, *The Lost Continent* starring Caesar Romero was indeed featured on the *Midnight Mystery Theater*, despite what *TV Guide* had indicated.

"Well? You believe me now?" Jeff asked Bobby by phone first thing the next morning.

"Can I get to meet him too?" Bobby asked, his snootiness gone.

"Sure. I guess. Well, I dunno," Jeff said, suddenly not so sure he wanted to share his privileged position and a possible big break in show business with anyone else. "I'll have to ask."

"When are you gonna see him again?"

"I dunno," Jeff said. "It's hard to say. Hey,

want to go to the Planetarium today?"

"Can't. Gotta go up to Stamford and visit my grandmother in the nursing home."

An hour later, Jeff was all prepared to go across town to the Planetarium by himself when the telephone rang and his mother said a little suspiciously, "It's some man calling for you."

"Renfield, my boy," said the voice at the end of the line.

"Zack!"

"Care to take in a movie this afternoon with the old nightstalker?"

"You mean you and me?"

"That's right."

"God! Sure. Where?"

They quickly ironed out the details

"Who was that?" his mother asked as soon as he hung up.

"Nobody," Jeff said.

"It must have been somebody."

"It was somebody I know, but nobody you know."

"I see," she said.

Jeff had agreed to meet the Count at the 55th Street Trans-Lux Theater on Lexington Avenue at noon. Naturally, he arrived there fifteen minutes early. Zack came five minutes late, wearing civilian clothes: khakis, loafers, a green crewneck sweater and old tweed coat with leather elbow patches. He also sported a beret, an article of clothing worn in that era only by beatniks, college students pretending to be beatniks, and Frenchmen. Zack bought two tickets and they went inside.

Even in the crepuscular dimness of the theater, Jeff sensed a deep gloom enveloping his hero, though the Count tried to maintain a jaunty air, cracking jokes all through the coming attractions. However, his long angular frame lay slouched way down in his seat, as though some terrible burden was weighing on him, and Jeff noticed him heave sighs between his jokes.

The show was a double feature. The opener, *Doctor Sardonicus*, featuring Oscar Homolka, was the tale of a fellow whose face froze into a horrible mask of fright upon opening the grave of his deceased beloved some years prior to the movie's setting. The character's mental health had declined since then and he now liked doing kinky things like putting leeches on wayward maidens who wandered up to his mansion. The Count gave the film a "one and a half bat" rating out of a possible four bats. The main attraction was a Technicolor remake of *The Mummy*. This one starred the redoubtable Christopher Lee in the role of Amenhotep. The Count awarded it three and half bats.

"What do you say we drop up to my own personal crypt?" the Count asked as they debouched back into the blinding October sunlight on Lexington Avenue, shielding their eyes against the glare like a couple of vampires.

"You mean, where you actually *live*?"

"If you call it living," the Count cracked with a gallows chuckle. "It's only three blocks away. There's something I want to show you."

"Gee. Okay. Sure."

Minutes later, they stood before an old brownstone on 53rd Street off Third Avenue. There was a Chinese laundry on the ground floor. Though hardly an experienced judge of Manhattan real estate, Jeff sensed that the address lacked something in the way of luster, and the trek up four dusty flights of stairs to the Count's apartment reinforced that impression. Zack unlocked the door with three different keys and they entered. It was a studio apartment, tidy, but pitifully under-furnished by the standard to which Jeff was accustomed. An old sofa was pushed up under two windows that looked out on a bleak courtyard festooned with lines of laundry. There was a battered card table with two folding chairs. Several cardboard cartons were filled with articles of clothing, shirts in one, socks in another, and so on. The walls were decorated with museum prints of impressionist paintings, chiefly Monet and Degas. Jeff was astounded to find no posters of horror movies, nor even any magazine cut-outs, like those that plastered his own room. One wall, however, was entirely covered with little notes from various magazines — *The New Yorker, Esquire, The Saturday Evening Post*. They appeared to be brief thank-you notes. But most astonishing of all to Jeff was the bathtub located in the middle of the tiny kitchen. It seemed like a practical joke.

"Do you actually take baths in there?"

"Every century or so," the Count said jauntily,

tossing his beret on the card table.

"Is this what you wanted to show me?"

"Heavens no. I thought I'd read you one of my short stories, if you don't mind listening."

"God… Jeez. I'd be happy to."

Jeff took a seat on the sagging sofa while the Count rummaged through a cardboard carton. He eventually extracted a typed manuscript that looked as though it had passed through many hands. On the title page, Jeff observed, was a brownish ring where somebody had set a coffee cup. The Count sat in one of the folding chairs and began to read the story. It was titled, "To Be Young and in Love in Paris."

Jeff had a hunch from the outset that it might not be about the kinds of things in which he was interested, and this turned out to be largely correct, though he gave the piece his complete attention. Nor did the Count read it with the customary flair of his TV persona, but rather in a subdued, breathless voice. As near as Jeff could make out, it was the tale of a young American named Charles who was crazy about a French girl named Giselle who had another boyfriend named Antoine. Charles did many outrageous things to impress Giselle, like jumping into the Seine River with his clothes on. A lot of the action took place at a cafe where Giselle worked as a waitress. Jeff was struck by the number of times the characters paused to light cigarettes, or "dragged thoughtfully" on them between lines of dialogue. In the end, Antoine wins the girl. Charles hangs a big banner from the Eiffel Tower that says *Charles will always love Giselle*, only in French, and departs Paris for the States, sadder but wiser.

When he was finished, the Count stacked up the dog-eared pages and then sat almost primly with the story in his lap. Jeff properly sensed that his hero was waiting for a response.

"God, that was great," he said. "How'd you ever learn so much about France?"

"I was there once," the Count said, "a long time ago."

"Did you do crazy things like this Charles guy?"

"No," the Count said with a wistful sigh. "I suppose that's why I had to write this story. Oh, well. What do you say we head over to Schrafft's for a hot fudge sundae?"

"Jeez. Yeah. Sure."

But the Count remained gloomy and preoc-
cupied at Schrafft's on 57th Street and they ate
their sundaes silently until Jeff couldn't stand it
anymore. Being a clever child, but nonetheless
innocent about the sorrows and vexations of adult-
hood, he thought it best to breach the silence by
choosing a subject tied to his own self-interest.

"Hey, Zack?"

"Yes?"

"Remember that day we went to the Automat?"

"As though it were yesterday."

"And you said that maybe I might fit in on
your show?"

"Yes?"

"Well, do you think I still might? I could
play Janos. I could! I can do the whole Transylvania accent and everything. And it would be a
million times better than just a stuffed dummy.
Whaddaya say? Want to give me a try? I could do
it, I swear. I can be funny!"

"I'm sure you can," the Count said. "But to tell
you the truth, things are. . . a little unsettled over
at the station right now."

"Unsettled?"

"They're kind of ticked off at me."

"Because of the Automat?"

"No. Not that."

"How come then?"

"Oh, they weren't too pleased about me switching the movies. The *TV Guide* people called up and made a big fuss. It's nothing you need to worry about."

Jeff was stricken. He put down his spoon and gaped across the crisp white tablecloth at the Count, whose expression seemed oddly pained.

"They're not gonna fire you, are they?"

"Fire *me*?" the Count recoiled theatrically as the manic gleam of his TV persona flashed in his eyes. "Why, the only way they'll ever get rid of me," he exclaimed loudly, causing heads to turn all around them, "is with a silver bullet!"

Jeff's hopes for joining the cast of the *Midnight Mystery Theater* and becoming the envy of P.S.6 were thus deferred. In fact, after saying good-bye to his friend and hero outside Schrafft's late that Saturday afternoon, he didn't hear from the Count all week. What's more, he was dogged by a

sense of guilt that he had somehow been respon-
sible for the Count's problems at the station —
that had he not snuck out of the house that fateful
Friday night and barged in on his idol none of
these difficulties would have ever come about, not
the escapade in the Automat, about which Phil
was so ticked off, nor the unscheduled showing
of *The Lost Continent*, none of it. And weighed
down by these regrets and self-recriminations,
Jeff did not tell his best friend Bobby Schindler
about how the Count personally took him to the
movies, or how he went over to the Count's own
personal crypt on 53rd Street, or how they went
out for sundaes at Schrafft's afterwards.

Now the following Friday happened to be that
favorite holiday of young persons all across
America: Halloween. Jeff and Bobby had made
elaborate preparations for the great evening. The
only question, really, was whose building they
would do their trick-or-treating in. It was ultimate-
ly decided to do it in Bobby's, which had seven-
teen stories to Jeff's twelve, and therefore was

arithmetically better-suited for collecting large amounts of candy and UNICEF money.

Jeff, in full costume and makeup, headed over to Bobby's at five o'clock, while it was still light out and Madison Avenue bustled with grownups returning from work in Midtown and visiting the neighborhood's purveyors of lamb chops, dry-cleaning, charlotte russes, and gin. Depending on their dispositions, the passers-by regarded the misbegotten hunchbacked, one-eyed, scarified, orange-haired, dwarf ape boy who loped in their midst with either disgust or amusement.

Bobby, in contrast, was garbed in the white lab coat, bottle-thick eyeglasses and fake buck teeth of a mad scientist, and would proclaim himself at each apartment they visited as the "keeper" of the gibbering wretch portrayed by Jeff, explaining that contributions to UNICEF could halt such terrible birth defects in the future (and that candy in lieu of cash payment was acceptable). Their night's work netted nine pounds of assorted goodies and $23.25 each.

At ten o'clock, Bobby's mother put Jeff in a taxicab home. It took him almost an hour to get off all his makeup and the rubber scars that he'd glued on and to shower the orange highlights out of his hair, but by 11:30 he was snug in his warm little tomb with only the local news and weather to endure before *Count Zackuloff's Midnight Mystery Theater* would crackle over the airwaves. This special Halloween night, *TV Guide* said, the program would feature that seminal work of cinema horror, the original *Frankenstein* starring Colin Clive as the Doctor, Boris Karloff as his doomed creature, and the immortal Dwight Frye as Renfield.

As the program opened, the Count appeared in his familiar dungeon-like set, and he engaged in the usual preparatory antics that delighted so many of his fans — visiting Hortense in her packing crate, chasing Janos around the set, and lip-synching a number from his new album, "The Moon, Your Neck, and You." But when it was time for *Frankenstein* to come on, something rather strange happened: in its place appeared opening credits for the musical *Rose Marie* starring Nelson Eddy and Jeanette MacDonald. The ridiculous operetta had not been on for more than three minutes when the Count interrupted it and materialized on camera in a blonde wig pretending to sing Miss MacDonald's part. Then the movie returned for a while. Then the Count returned wearing a Royal Canadian Mounted Police hat lip-synching Mr. Eddy's part. This switching back-and-forth went on for perhaps a quarter of an hour altogether until, during one of those intervals when the Count was caterwauling in his blonde wig, the screen went blank. Sounds of a scuffle could be heard briefly. Finally, a test pattern lit the screen, accompanied by a painful electronic wail. Jeff turned off the annoying sound but kept the picture on, watching the test pattern anxiously. But neither the Count nor Nelson Eddy nor Jeanette MacDonald nor any movie returned to the Channel Five airwaves that Halloween night.

Bobby called first thing the next morning.

"Did you see what that crazy Count did last night?"

"Uh-huh," Jeff replied gloomily.

"Was that weird, or what? Betcha they fire him for it."

"They can't fire him. He's the only thing anybody watches on that stupid excuse for a TV station."

"Then how come they pulled the plug on him last night?"

"How do I know. Maybe their camera broke."

"I betcha he got the axe. Hey, want to go down to Abercrombie and Fitch's and play with all the stuff on the first floor?"

"No."

"Want to come over here and lob stuff off the terrace? My Mom's got root canal the whole afternoon."

"I don't feel like it."

"Want to go see that new version of *The Mummy* down at the Trans-Lux?"

"I, uh, I don't think so."

"It's a double bill with this thing called *Doctor Sardonicus*. I heard he puts leaches on his victims."

"Some other time, maybe."

"Okay, *be* a sorehead," Bobby said and hung up.

In fact, it started raining later that morning and Jeff did little beside mope around his tomb all day. Before dinnertime, he was inspired to call the information operator at the phone company and obtain the number for one Z. Orloff on East 53rd Street, but nobody answered all night long until it was time for Jeff to go to bed. Nor did anyone answer Sunday morning. That afternoon, his father took him up to Yankee Stadium to see the Giants play the Green Bay Packers in one of the most important contests of the season, but Jeff could hardly wait for the game to end. Sunday night, he tried the Count's number a few more times without results. Finally, the long, painful weekend drew to a close and he lay in bed with the reading light on surrounded by his old friends, the famous monsters of filmland, thinking that maybe it was time to put up pictures of President Kennedy and rocket ships instead.

Monday his spirits lifted somewhat. Mrs. Snipes was out sick and they had a substitute teacher who showed a movie in the morning (*Around the World for UNICEF* — narrated by Danny Kaye — which featured footage of people from foreign lands with incredible diseases), and in the afternoon they held a spelling bee. At three o'clock, the little inmates of P.S. 6 were released from their classrooms into a gorgeous Indian summer day, with the thermometer kissing sixty degrees. Jeff and Bobby had just decided to fetch their bikes and go over to Central Park when a riot of squealing erupted at mid-block down Madison and Jeff heard a familiar voice crying, "Renfield! Renfield!" rise above all the squealing. He wheeled to see the startling figure of Count Zackuloff in full regalia and ghostly makeup looming above the heads of his classmates as they proffered scraps of loose-leaf paper and clamored for autographs. "Renfield, my boy!"

"Zack!" Jeff bellowed, and fought his way past the other children to his hero's side.

"This way," the Count said. "I've a cab waiting on the corner of 81st."

"Where are we going?"

"Someplace special. You'll see."

"Can I come too?" asked Bobby, who had likewise squirmed through the mob.

The Count patted him on the head, saying, "Sorry, sonny, but Renfield and I have business to discuss."

The Count managed to clear a path to the corner for himself and Jeff, who, by now, was convinced that some miracle of show business had occurred to favorably resolve the Count's problems down at Channel Five — perhaps that the petty, humorless, chain-smoking Phil Torgesen had been fired by the station's bosses and the Count had forced them to sign up Jeff to portray Janos, and that the two of them were now triumphantly en route to the studio to begin rehearsals for Friday's show. He was going to be a star after all…!

"Take us over to the zoo, driver," the Count said, once they settled inside the cab.

"What's over at the zoo?" Jeff asked.

"Animals," the Count replied mysteriously and smiled. When the cab swung around onto Fifth Avenue, the Count began wiping his make-up off with a pack of tissues. At the entrance to the zoo on 64th Street, Zack paid the driver, but before they got out, he unpinned the Royal Transylvanian Star of Skullduggery from his boiled shirtfront and handed it to Jeff, saying, "Here, you keep this."

Jeff clasped the large jewel-bedizened medal

tightly in his fist, beginning to apprehend an unraveling of his hopes and dreams. Out on the sidewalk, the Count put on his beret and donned sunglasses. Except for the black moldy suit, he looked nearly like an ordinary person.

"What do you say we look in on our kinsmen, the great apes?" he said.

"Okay."

The zoo was sparsely attended at this hour on a Monday. The building that housed the gorillas and orangutans also contained a contingent of ragtag lions, tigers, and an elderly black panther held in captivity so long that it had developed the dolorous habit of banging its head against the wall of its cage. The male gorilla sat on an upper wooden platform sucking daintily at a Sugar Daddy lollipop that someone had tossed through the bars. Its mate lolled right up beside the bars silently eyeing the zoo-goers with an expression of mild contempt. Zack hung morosely over the rail that separated the cage from the public, his long arms dangling, while Jeff peered under the rail. The building stank ferociously.

"Am I going to get the part or what?" Jeff finally mumbled, as much to end the excruciating silence as to receive an answer.

"I've been sacked," the Count said quietly.

"You what?"

"I've been sacked. Canned, cashiered, dis-missed, terminated, let go... fired."

"Oh God," Jeff groaned.

"No, it's really better this way."

"But. . . but who'll be the Count?"

"The Count," Zachary Orloff said portentously, staring the female gorilla straight in the eyes, "is no more."

The fetid air in the place made Jeff's head swim. He felt suddenly sick to his stomach.

"He can't just die."

"He will always live...in our memories."

Jeff reared back and punched his former hero in the arm, and then in the side, and the hip and the leg, screaming, "Why did you have to go and ruin it for, you crazy jerk!"

"Hey, Renfield, hey—"

"And quit calling me Renfield!"

"Okay, okay. Only will you please stop hitting me."

"No."

Zack stood there and allowed Jeff to swing

away until Jeff appeared to exhaust himself. Finally, with reddened eyes and slimy goop running out of one nostril, Jeff turned back to the gorillas and said almost inaudibly, "A lot of people are going to miss the old Count."

"No, they're not."

"Yes, they are."

"Do you know what the average TV watcher out there is like?"

"Like me," Jeff said. "I'm average."

"No, you're not. The average TV watcher is like Missus Kong here. Imagine what it's like playing the Count for thousands of people like that?"

Jeff gazed at the gorilla. He had never before tried to imagine the blankness of mind behind those human-like eyes, and the idea that some kind of mental abyss occupied the beast's skull rather spooked him. "So, what are you going to do now, anyway?" Jeff asked glumly.

"Go back to Massachusetts for a while. Try to write some more short stories," Zack said, adding emphatically, "and sell them, too!"

"Like the story about that guy Charles in Paris?"

"That's right."

"You'll never sell a story like that," Jeff said. "That story stunk."

Zack recoiled and made a face that was distinctly un-Countlike. "I'll get better with a little practice," he said in a tone of voice that, to Jeff, for the first time in their acquaintance, sounded less than whole-heartedly self-assured.

"Can we get out of here and go visit the seals or something?" Jeff said. "This place smells."

"Sure," Zack agreed and, as they headed for the door, the black panther began banging its head against the wall.

Jeff felt a little better out in the sunshine and fresh air. The seals basked lazily atop their cement lodgings in the large pool at the zoo's center.

"If you have to be a writer, can't you at least try writing a few horror stories instead of that Paris stuff?"

"I suppose I can give it a try," Zack said. "You know, it's a good thing the two of us met when we did."

"It was a disaster."

"No, really. You've been a good friend. About the best since I came to New York."

"You've got to be kidding."

"No, I'm serious. You can't imagine what a lonely place this city is."

Zack was quite correct. Jeff couldn't imagine. To him, New York was, if anything, too cluttered with parents, relatives, friends of his parents, friends of his own, schoolmates and whole classes of citizens with whom one had no choice but to coexist cheek by jowl. "Aw Jeez," was all he could summon in reply.

They lingered beside the seal pool a few more minutes. The sun stole behind the elephant house and the evening's seasonal chill began to assert itself. Jeff scribbled his address on a piece of loose-leaf paper so Zack could mail him a horror story as soon as he finished one. Finally, Zack walked Jeff back to Fifth Avenue. When the first uptown bus came along, they shook hands and said goodbye.

Jeff Greenaway's fame as the friend and confident of Count Zackuloff endured, within the reasonable limit of children's' memories — say a month or so.

But forever after that fateful Halloween show, the Channel Five *Midnight Mystery Theater* was broadcast without any host, just straight horror movies and commercials. Somehow a strange rumor briefly spread around P.S. Six that the Count was Jeff's father, but this story was quickly squelched by Bobby Schindler and other loyal friends who had actually met Kenneth Greenaway in the flesh and could avouch that he was nothing more frightful than a Wall Street lawyer.

The *Transylvania Times* ceased publication and the denizens of that faraway realm lost their hold on Jeff's imagination. As the fall skipped away brightly into the long Yuletide, when the city is at its most enchanting, Jeff began to conceive an inordinate fascination with the world of professional wrestling, whose colorful brutes and behemoths could be seen in combat every Wednesday night on Channel 11. Before long, photos of Haystack Calhoun, Killer Kowalski, the Masked Marvel, and the Fabulous Kangaroo Brothers were plastered on the wall beside his bed where lately Lugosi, Chaney, and Karloff had glowered.

Through the long winter that followed, with its several snowstorms and great sledding on nearby Cherry Hill in Central Park, Jeff received no short stories in the mail from Zachary Orloff in Massachusetts. But in March he got a card postmarked *Seattle* bearing the familiar ghoul's grinning countenance and this printed announcement: "Station KWSH proudly introduces *Count Zackuloff's Midnight Madness* beginning April 3." Penned in the margin was this message: "You were right. Real career resumed. I'll be back. Stay young. Your pal, Zack."

A wicked smile crept over Jeff's face when he read the card and absorbed its contents. It was gratifying to be right about something in this world of parents, teachers, and casual scolds, with which New York was so well-supplied. He intended to stay young, for a while, anyway. Unless the alternative couldn't be avoided.

The End

www.ingramcontent.com/pod-product-compliance
Lightning Source LLC
Chambersburg PA
CBHW020604130626
46552CB00007B/3031